The Life of a Zombie

By David Evans

Table of Contents

Chapter 1: It Begins

A couple was vacationing on an island near the Marshall Islands, they were staying in an elaborate resort and planned on staying there for a few weeks to relax. They hired a tour guide to show them around the island, he led them down a path through the jungle until they came to a waterfall.

The couple stood in front of the falls and gave there camera to the guide to take their picture. Suddenly someone touched her on the shoulder, she screamed and ran over to the guide. Her boyfriend had a perplexed look on his face, and walked over to her.

"What happened Desiree?"

"Someone touched me on the shoulder."

I don't see anyone there now, I'm telling you there's someone there. The guide looked at her boyfriend and said I wouldn't go in there If I were you.

"Why not?"

"Because everyone who goes in there never comes out."

I'm not sure if I believe you, then go in the cave if you want. Don't be so stubborn my dear, listen to the man, he knows this island better then you do.

"Sir do you have a gun on you?"

"No," I left my gun at the resort.

"Did you hear that groan coming from the cave?"

"Yes," we did.

A rock came flying out of the cave and hit the tour guide. That's it I'm going in there, and his girlfriend held him back.

"Are the both of you coming?"

"Yes"

In an authoritative voice the guide said no one's allowed out at night.

"What's the reason for that?"

"Because there are dangerous animals that come out at night."

"Like what kind?"

"Leopards, baboons."

If you go out and shoot these animals you will be jailed, they're currently on their protected species list.

"Who do you think lives in that cave?"

"A ship wrecked hippie."

The last guide that was working here wandered out of his room at midnight because he heard something stirring in the forest, and he never came back.

"Was his body ever found?"

"No," it wasn't.

"How many baboons do you think live on this island?"

"100 of them."

"Where are you taking us now?"

"To see the ruins of oponok."

I take all of my visitors to these ruins, and they find the ruins to be interesting. Eventually they came upon the ruins, these ruins aren't very impressive to me. I don't think we'll be taking pictures of these boring ruins, your girlfriend is checking them out and you should too.

Go ahead over there by your girlfriend and I'll take your picture again, I appreciate the offer but I'm not interested. Fred saw something out of the corner of his eye, he quickly ran over to the guide. I saw something out of the corner of my eye, you shouldn't worry it was probably just a baboon.

Whatever it was it just ran behind that tree, that's not how a primate would act. His girlfriend came walking over to him, I saw a worried look on your face and I wanted to come over to see what was wrong. The tour guide walked towards the tree, and it ran away from the tree when it saw him coming and he got a good glimpse at it. The guide quickly ran over to the couple, I finally saw it and it was ugly.

"Describe to us what it looked like?"

"It was a man with blood all over his face and his skin was hanging off his body."

You need to have private security brought in here, before someone else goes missing like us. I'm not sure the owner of this place would like to bring in security on this island then he's crazy or something. You should say to him that your life is in danger, yes but that's not true.

I'm not comfortable with lying to get things changed around here. If my girlfriend and I go missing people will be coming out to look for us. From what you described to me it sounds like it's zombie, if you'd like I can let you borrow my gun tonight. I can't believe that my boyfriend would have said that, he's never shot a gun in his life.

How dare you tell the guide that, he didn't need to know that. He'd probably end up shooting himself instead of the zombie, don't say that you don't know that. The guide turned away from them and walked over to his truck, and started it up and drove it over to them.

Hop in and we'll go back to the resort, the man's girlfriend had an angered look on her face. We finally get to go on vacation and then this happens, I'm never going to let you book our next vacation again. You can't blame all of this on me, yes I can.

"Are the both of you going to argue the whole time we're in this truck?"

"No."

The both of you are talking so loud that you need to tone it down. Fred winked at his girlfriend, and said we'll talk about this later. Then she ignored the both of them and rolled her eyes and looked out the window. Once they got back to the resort, none of them could believe what had happened to it.

Some windows were smashed and the main entrance door was torn off its hinges, I don't think one zombie could do all this damage, there's probably more than one around here. I want the both of you to stay in this truck until I get back, I'll let you know what I find when I get back.

"Babe do you think the zombies are still in there?"

"Yes," I do.

Fred leaned forward and kissed his girlfriend on the cheek, you're just kissing me to suck up to me because you know that I'm angry. The next thing that you're probably going to do is bring me flowers, and I don't want any.

Fred turned on his smart phone and went into the home security app, to see what was going on back home. His girlfriend looked back at him, you go on that phone far too often. You should put that thing away while I'm talking to you, you have no room to talk you do the same thing to me. I've been thinking, you haven't bought me anything for a while.

"What's with the long face?"

"I'm feeling a bit stressed."

You should be happy that you're away from your desk, and not answering calls every minute. When we first met you always made time for me, and we had good times together.

Every time it's your birthday I always take you out for dinner, and give you a small gift. I'm getting tired of being taken out for dinner, and I'm tired of small gifts.

Just a week ago I took you out to the comedy club, and you haven't talked about that. I'm not even sure if you enjoyed that at all, I most certainly did.

Look at that baboon over there, his girlfriend had her head turned away from the window. You weren't answering me so I guess you're ignoring me again.

I'll look out the window when I want to, the monkey jumped up on the hood the truck. His girlfriend was now looking at the monkey, I don't like that this monkey is looking at us.

Just leave the monkey alone, he's not hurting anything. There's something behind that bush over there, I hope that it doesn't come this way. So what if it does we're inside the truck.

Fred got up into the front seat, I thought that you were going to stay back there. I came up here so that I would be closer to you, that's nice of you. I know of a gift that I could get you, I'll get you another necklace.

"Aren't you going to respond to that?"

"No," I'm not.

I really want to shoo this monkey away, don't worry about him just stay here with me. A zombie just walked past the broken window, I don't think the guide survived in there for very long. He should have waited until the zombies left, now he's a zombie.

"Do you think the zombies know were in this truck?"

"No," they don't.

"Where do you think we'll be sleeping tonight?"

"Where you're at right now."

I've never slept in a vehicle before, then this will be your first time. If I'm going to sleep in here then I'll need a pillow, I don't know what to say to you because I'm not going out there at least not right now. If I can sleep without a pillow you can do, I hope that my neck doesn't get kinked. It won't if you sleep correctly, I'd feel better if I had a gun in my hand right now.

"What are you trying to do with your hand?"

"Hold your hand."

I'm not so mad now so you can hold my hand, I like when we hold hands. We haven't held hands like this in two days. Sometimes you aren't always a good boyfriend, I can't believe you didn't say anything back to me just now. That's because I'm deep in thought, I'm wondering how we're going to get out of here.

You just keep on talking endlessly, if we don't get out of here we may never see the light of day again. That monkey finally got off of the truck, and now one of the zombies are chasing it.

"Do you think the zombie is going to catch up to it?"

"No"

I think that we should seek shelter on the roof of the resort, I think that's out of the question. You shoot down my ideas so quickly, just hear me out for a moment.

I see a way for us to get up there, there's a rope ladder hanging down from the roof in front of us. Sooner or later those zombies are going to break into this truck, I think it'll be awhile until they break into this truck. Truck and car windows aren't that hard to break, zombies won't feel any pain when they break their hands through the glass. Amazingly one of the zombies caught up with the monkey, and when the zombie walked past them it was holding the monkey. I think the zombie is trying to tell us that we're next. The question is which one of us is going to get out first.

"What are you looking for under the seat?"

"A gun."

I highly doubt that you'll find a gun under there, you're right there's no gun under there. I found a bottle of water, and a pencil. Look in the rearview mirror, the both zombies are now in the bed of the truck. They're getting closer to us, and are trying to break through the cab window.

They both swung open the doors and ran over to the ladder and began climbing up it. Whatever you do don't look back, stay focused on climbing. I'm just glad that were on the roof, I was afraid that the ladder was going to give way. Suddenly 12 monkeys came out of the forest, the zombies saw the monkeys and growled at them.

The zombies got themselves out of the truck and began walking towards the monkeys. Our guide just came walking out of the resort, I hope that he doesn't see us up here. He's got blood all over his shirt and is walking with a limp. He just walked over to the truck, and is looking inside the window.

Then maybe he's alright, I think that he's just trying to fool us. I find it rather peculiar that the zombies aren't going after him, something very strange is going on here. I'm starting to think that someone hired actors just to scare us, I only know of one friend who may have done this.

"Do you think that the monkeys are real?"

"Yes"

You must have drank some alcohol when I wasn't looking, I can promise you that I didn't. I haven't seen you drink anything for a while, here take a sip of water. Several monkeys just jumped on that one zombie knocking him down.

"Is the zombie trying to bite at the monkeys?"

"Yes," he is.

If the guide looks up here lay down and act like you're dead, don't be silly you don't need to do that. Now the zombies are rolling around on the ground with the monkeys. The guide turned around and walked over to the ladder, and climbed up until he reached the top.

You got a whole lot of explaining to do, I can explain. I can't believe what you did to us, you should be ashamed of yourself. I'm stressed out, and appalled, honey please stop yelling and calm yourself. If you don't stop talking you won't be able to hear him talking, I'm sorry that my boyfriend so rudely interrupted you, go ahead and speak now.

Chapter 2: Explanation

"They're real zombies, but they're not killers."

"Then why were they going after the monkeys?"

"Because they eat them"

"Can they talk?"

"Yes"

"How did they become zombies?"

"They had a spell placed on them"

"Who put it on them?"

"The island sorcerer."

They stole from him, they both took a piece of his gold. They told me that they died several days later and were buried, and at midnight they came alive again and got themselves out of the ground.

They said that they were starving and had come upon some monkeys, and caught one, killing it and eating it. I tried to teach them how to brush their teeth, but they didn't want to. Don't tell them to play dead or they will bury themselves.

They can't say the whole word monkey so they say monk. Don't say to them your dead to me, or they will ask who's dead and roll around on the ground. One of the jokes that they tell is what did the zombie say to the chicken? You're fast food. I'm not excited to meet them, his girlfriend and the guide climbed down the ladder, but Fred just stayed sitting. Come on dear, stop throwing a tantrum and come down here with us. You look ridiculous up there, I bet you'll come down here if I take the ladder away.

I'll have one of the zombies come up here then, you go ahead and do that. I'll just push him off the roof when he gets up here, those zombies also need to give me their apologies. I doubt that they can, if I was down there right now you wouldn't like what I would do to them.

The guide introduced his girlfriend to the zombies, this is zombie 1 and that's zombie 2 over there. Don't shake their hands just look into their eyes for a minute, I can't tell what color their eyes are anymore. The last person that shook their hands almost made them fall off.

I'm not even sure if that zombie heard what I said to him, then repeat to him what you said. It was nice to meet you zombie 1, and the zombie shook it's head. He's sure a zombie of few words, your boyfriend is missing all of this. That's okay maybe he'll go into a dream, and leave me alone.

"Will zombie 2 come over here if I whistle?"

"No."

I'll just go to get him for you then. He brought zombie 2 over near her, the zombie was gritting his teeth.

"Is he mad when he does that?"

"No," he's just nervous.

Zombie 2 told me that he wants to tell you a joke, I hope that it's a good clean joke.

"What holiday does a zombie celebrate?"

"I'm not sure."

That's not an answer I'll accept.

"Is it Halloween?"

"No," but good guess.

We celebrate "The Day Of The Dead."

"What do they say to a zombie when he's wrong?"

"That he's brain dead, that's close."

"That he's dead wrong, that's silly."

"Do zombies dream?"

"Yes."

I've had several nightmares that I was lost on a dead end street. While I was buried a worm became my friend, that's the weirdest thing I've heard in a while. Eventually her boyfriend came down off the roof, the zombies looked over at him. I don't like how those zombies are standing so close to you.

It's okay dear, they're not going to devour me or something. The zombie is telling me funny jokes, and being kind to me. Her boyfriend walked over to the guide, I could really use a cigar right about now. It's been a long time since I've had a cigar, answered the guide.

Listen to me zombie man you better not lay your hands on her, or I'll slam you into the ground. You don't have to talk so wicked to him, this zombie is behaved.

"Does this resort have a gift shop?"

"No," it don't.

The owner of this property will be building a gift shop next year. He really shouldn't be waiting that long to build the shop.

"Do you know what they're going to be selling at the gift shop?"

"No"

They should give everyone that's an adult that comes here a cigar. Suddenly a swarm of giant flying insects came flying in, Fred and his girlfriend went running for cover inside the resort, the guide dove under his truck.

Zombie 1 and 2, ran into the jungle to take cover, but still several of the bugs were after them. Zombie 1 found a stick and started hitting the bugs, which only made them angrier. Zombie 2 started throwing rocks at the bugs, this caused one of the bugs to fall to the ground.

Both zombies ran out of the forest, and made a beeline for the resort. They quickly got inside and closed the door behind them, they looked at one another and laughed. They found the others in the safe room, sitting down on a couch talking.

They had disregarded the guide who was still under his truck, they heard a loud crash on the roof. Fred and his girlfriend were embracing one another, I'm afraid that they're going to get through the roof. It's highly unlikely, that they're going to find a way to get in here.

The guides going to be mad at us for not helping him, who knows what may have happened to us if we stayed out there with them bugs flying around.

"Did you get a good look at those bugs?"

"No."

"What about you?"

"I got a glimpse of them"

they had four wings and resembled dragon flies, but what was odd was they had a scorpion tail on them. I wonder why they didn't come after us while we were in the jungle hours ago, maybe they were out scavenging for food during that time.

"What do you think they're eating?"

"Anything that they can find"

Meanwhile outside several of the bugs were flying around the truck looking for a means to get at the guide. The guide looked around frantically for something he could use to defend himself against the bugs, but there was nothing there. The bugs began hissing at him, and several of the largest bugs in sheer determination wrapped their legs around the truck and we're trying to lift it up.

This only made the guide, more nervous and he was trembling in fear. 1 of the flying bugs landed on the ground, and began crawling towards him.

Eventually the bugs lifted up the truck, once they did the guide got himself up and ran for the entrance of the resort and quickly swung open the door and closed it behind him.

The bugs crawled up to the door and began violently slamming into it, a large crack developed in the wall. He feverishly ran down the hall until he reached the safe room, I'm so glad to see everyone again. Both zombies walked over to him and gave him a hug, and mumbled to him you're safe now.

Thanks zombies you got blood all over my shirt, but I shouldn't be complaining about a thing. Fred got up and began rooting around in the nearby closet, I can't find anything in this closet that will help defend us against those bugs out there.

Hopefully we'll all be able to get in the truck and drive away from here, I'm afraid that we won't be able to do that. The bugs carried it away, and who knows where it is now. These bugs are driving me out of my mind, I don't know what we're going to do.

His girlfriend got up and put her hand on his shoulder, I can feel the tension in your body dear. You should take a seat and let the guide figure out a plan, you know that I'm not lazy and that I don't really like relying on others.

Settle yourself then a plan will come to your mind, believe me I know that we're in a tent situation at the moment. I feel like we're locked in here like prisoners at a jail, things have to get better now.

"Which one of you are willing to take a risk for me?"

"One of the zombies raised his arm and said I will."

The zombie limped over to Fred, I'm ready at your command. The second zombie made his way over to Fred, and he had headphones on his head and sunglasses on. You look like a cool dude with those headphones and shades on, you're starting to look less like a zombie.

I doubt that he could hear anything I said to him, just let him go dear. He's probably never had headphones or sunglasses on, just let him enjoy himself. Fred handed a walking stick over to zombie one, use this to defend yourself. Zombie two quickly grabbed the stick from zombie one and hit Fred with it. That was very uncalled for, I didn't do anything to you. My girlfriend just stood up for you and you did that, I should throw you out with the bugs.

"What are you doing zombie 1?"

"I'm trying to dance."

I've never seen someone dance the way you do. The zombie twisted his body around and fell down, the guide helped him up. Here's the plan everyone, if we go out and if the bugs are there were going to throw flaming walking sticks at them.

I found 2 more walking sticks, and a bottle of gasoline and a rag. Fred gave everyone a stick and he carried the bottle of gasoline and rag. They left the safe room and went to the entrance, there was a hole through the wall. Fred opened the door and walked out and soon after the bugs came back.

His girlfriend handed him a lighter, and kissed him on the cheek. He poured some gasoline on the stick, and lit it up with the lighter. When the bugs got close to him, he threw the stick at them. Several of them caught fire, and fell down. One of the zombies came running out, and started beating the bugs that were on the ground.

  "What you doing out here zombie 1?"

  "Helping you to beat up the bugs."

  "Did zombie 2 tell you why he hit me earlier?"

  "He said that you made him angry."

  "Do you figure that we got them all?"

  "Yes," I do.

Watch out zombie 1 there's a giant snake, coming down off of the roof. You should stay very still so that it doesn't see you, lucky for you it's going the other direction. Don't stand so far away from me, you never know what else is lurking out there. They high fived one another, and walked back into the resort.

You both did a great job out there, and that was an enormous snake. You should have went after it, we couldn't have done that. They all spent the evening together, and soon fell asleep. The next day the couple left the island and several hours later they were home.

Meanwhile in Kenya a great mystery occurred, there haven't been many reports about what had happened. Dakarai is an explorer and is a hunter, he prefers to go on long hunting trips all by himself.

He's an excellent tracker and prefers to hunt with a bolt action rifle. He takes good care of his rifle, while he's out in the wilderness he brings along a large hunting knife and his rifle and a canteen full of fresh water.

One time while Dakarai was hunting, he was approached by a cape buffalo. Luckily Dakarai saw the buffalo before it charged him and kneeled down behind a boulder, the buffalo didn't even know that he was there. He saw that there were some trees off to his right so he slowly walked over by the trees.

He hid behind the trees. He looked around for a while and noticed that there was a herd of elephants approaching him from behind. There were two huge mighty bull elephants in the front of the herd.

One of the bull elephants had a scar near his right eye. He must have been attacked by another bull elephant. The ground shook from the weight of the elephants. Dust was flying up and all around the herd of elephants.

Suddenly the herd of elephants stopped walking and began to feed on the grass and shrubs that were beneath their feet. Dakarai kept his eyes on the herd of elephants. Towards the back of the herd, there was a baby elephant alongside his mother. The baby elephant had short stubby legs.

He wasn't well balanced and would topple over, his mother would take her trunk and lift him back up when he would fall. The bull elephant with the scar near his eye remained on edge. The female elephants seemed to stay near the very back of the herd. Dakarai was getting tired of staying so still but realized if he moved he would probably be noticed by one of the bull elephants.

He saw someone out of the corner of his eye, he thought to himself who's crazy enough to be running around out here. Then the person walked out in front of him, it was a man with blood running down his face and was missing part of his ear and walked with a limp. His clothes were tore apart, and blood was coming out of his neck.

That's when he realized that this man was a zombie, he was scared and wasn't sure if he should talk to the man. There were flies swarming after the zombie but it ignored them. It turned and was now looking at him, and began mumbling something that he couldn't understand. He yelled speak up zombie, it spoke up and said I'm not going to harm you.

"How long have you been walking around out here?"

"Several weeks."

"Do you still feel pain?"

"No."

I was trying to make friends with the animals but all they want to do is take a bite out of me.

"Do you remember your name zombie?"

"No," I don't.

"Do you have any weapons on you?"

"No."

You should find your way back home, I can't remember where my house is. You should be hiding in a cave somewhere, not out here in the open savanna.

The zombie came towards him like he was going to give him a hug, I like talking to you but I don't want a hug. I don't wanna catch whatever you have, you sure do have some weird eyes.

That's not how my eyes used to be, it used to be blue. The sun has burn your forehead to a crisp, but I guess it don't matter to you. Dakarai took out his cell phone, and took a picture with the zombie.

Don't forget to say cheese, I don't understand what you mean. Forget about what I said just smile for me, you know that you only have 1 tooth in your mouth.

I didn't know that things were telling me, and the zombie walked away from him and waved goodbye to him. Suddenly a large mosquito flew over the top of Dakarai's head and began to buzz around his ear. The mosquito was an annoyance to Dakarai and soon tried to land on his arm.

He let out a yawn and kept on trying to keep the mosquito from landing on his bald head or neck. The mosquito kept on buzzing around him, as he waved his arms up in the air to chase it away.

Chapter 3: The Hunting Conversation

One of the bull elephants must have noticed him and it lifted up his trunk and let out a noise like he was alerting the rest of the herd. Then the second bull elephant pulled his ears back and seemed like he was going to charge him. This bull elephant looked like he was irritated that he was watching him.

Suddenly the bull elephant with the scar came charging closer to Dakarai got down onto his stomach and hid behind a tree. He was hoping that the bull elephant wouldn't charge him. He knew that if the elephant would charge that would have seconds to get out of the way or risk getting trampled on.

He knew that the tree he was hiding behind him wouldn't offer much protection against an angry charging bull elephant. However, he kept a round chambered in his rifle. His rifle was a single shot 500 express, this rifle was so powerful that he used it to take down a charging hippo last week.

Sometimes he'll take American hunters on dangerous game hunting trips. Over the years he has taken many American hunters on dangerous game hunting trips. The most memorable big game hunt for him was when he took an American hunter out on a leopard hunt.

All day the hunter and Dakarai were waiting to see a leopard come by. Dakarai had put out the carcass of a dead antelope and hung it up in a tree. Dakarai and the hunter waited there for 2 hours and still, no leopard came by. Dakarai couldn't understand what was going on.

"The hunter looked over at Dakarai"

"What's going on?"

"I honestly don't know, I've spent all of this money to come out Africa for a guided hunt for a leopard and then I wait all day and don't see a leopard."

It's not my fault the leopards aren't coming around, I don't know the leopard's schedule. You better figure it out soon or I'm going to call off this hunt. You live in Africa so you should know everything about the Wildlife down here. I live in the Texas, so I don't know much about the behavior of the leopards.

"Isn't there anything else you can do to attract them"

"Yes"

I can put more bait out and put some more blood around the bottom of the tree. You have to be patient, or you won't be able to shoot a one. I want to see at least one before the sun goes down. Leopards hunt their prey at night and maybe they will come out tonight and you will get a shot at one. Yes, the scope of my rifle isn't equipped for shooting at night.

The scope on my rifle is a long-range scope, and when it gets dark you can't see anything out of the scope. I understand that but my rifle has a night scope on it and I'm going to let you borrow my rifle for the night. That's very thoughtful of you to give me that choice.

"How long have you been putting on guided hunts?"

"I've been putting on guided hunts for three years"

"Did you ever get charged by a rhino before?"

"No," but I was charged once but a hippo.

"Where you near a watering hole when the hippo charged you?"

"No," I was on the savanna when the hippo charged me.

"Did he come at you very fast?"

"Yes," I had a second to take the shot.

"Where did the bullet hit the hippo?"

It was hard to tell, I had shot him right behind the neck and I was able to get another shot off at him and that bullet struck him right between his eyes.

"Did he collapse there in front of you?"

"He did"

If he would have been any closer he would have been on top of me, that must have been an eye-opening experience. It was but I've been running around the bush for my whole life, I'm not afraid of anything that prowls on the land.

"Did you ever guide a lion hunt?"

"No"

"I love lions and I don't like to see them shot."

"How much would it cost to go on a lion hunt?"

"I would have to check up on that."

"How much was the hippo hunt?"

"$60,000"

"Have you taken hunters on elephant hunts lately?"

"No," the last elephant hunt I was on with an American hunter was last year.

"Was that hunter like me?"

"He was a lot more patient then you are."

"Was that the only difference?"

"Yes"

"What's that animal called that's walking towards us?"

"That's a bushbuck, he doesn't look like the deer that I see in the United States."

Bushbucks are about the same size of a whitetail buck but their coloring is different. The hide on a bushbuck is much darker than the hide on a whitetail deer. These deer live their lives near the water's edge and feed on some of the aquatic plants, you're an interesting fellow who knows a lot about nature.

"Have you seen many giraffes out here?"

"I have but very rarely, my name is Kansas, it's nice to have met you."

"Do you think we're going to remain safe once it gets dark?"

"Yes," we'll be fine and I haven't been attacked by a leopard.

I like to watch nature, I used to be a photographer

"Why did you stop being a photographer?"

"I got bored of it and wanted to travel around the world on elaborate big game hunting trips."

It's almost dark and, there's no sign of a leopard anywhere.

"Did you hear that snarl coming from over there?"

"Yes," it sounds like a lion growling

"How many lions do you think there are in the area?"

"There's just one lion here at the moment."

"How comes there's a lion and no leopard?"

That's a good question.

"Here's my gun"

"Why are you handing me your gun?"'

"In case the lion decides to charge us."

"If a lion charged you, would you shoot him?"

"Yes," I would in self-defense.

I heard the growl again and it sounds like the lion is getting closer to us.

"Where do you figure the growl in coming from?"

"The lion must be out in front of us somewhere."

Let's just hope that the lion doesn't charge us.

"What if the lion charges us?"

"I'll take him down with one bullet."

"Do you think the lion is a male or female?"

"The lion's probably a male just scavenging around for an easy meal."

"What are we going to do with the lion's body if we have to shoot him?"

"I'll take care of that, just keep focused on your hunt."

Don't let one lion ruin your evening, I can see the lion from here

"What are we going to do now?"

"Just let the lion go and don't bother him."

I wasn't planning on bothering the lion, there seems to be something wrong with that lion.

"Why do you say that?"

"He's walking around in a circle, maybe he found some food and is looking for some more scraps to eat."

He's a beautiful male lion Kansas, he looks like he's healthy, except for the blood that's all over his mange.

"You really think lions are beautiful?"

"Yes"

There aren't many lions left in the wild, I don't think lions are beautiful. I consider them as being cruel killing machines, lions have to kill to survive. Look, the lion's approaching the bait, it's creepy how the lion keeps looking over at us.

I know but it's nothing to worry about, as long as we stay still and don't make a movement the lion won't know that were here. I don't believe that though, I think that the lion might be able to smell us. Yes, I am sure that the lion can smell us. That's why he keeps on looking at us.

I was on my computer the other day and I read an article about a group of hunters that were attacked and killed by a wild lion. They had a picture of the lion in the article, that lion really closely resembles the one in the article. I'm afraid that it may be the same one. It has the same markings as the lion in the picture.

I don't feel that were safe here anymore. I'm here and I'll risk my life for you. I know that you're paying good money for this hunt and I want you to have good memories. If you want me to have good memories then you can go get me a leopard. I can't just go and get you a leopard, that's not how it works.

I'll do all that I can to find you a leopard but it won't be easy. I realize that since the lion is here, were going to have to wait until he leaves for a leopard to come by.

> "Why's that?"

> "Leopards are afraid of lions and that's just how it is. I think that we should just call off this hunt and I'll go home broken-hearted."

I refuse to give up this hunt over a stray lion, that's no stray lion. He's a man-eater and I want to shoot him. You don't have a tag for a lion, so that means that you can only shoot a leopard. I don't care about the laws, and you shouldn't either.

I care about my profession and don't want any trouble with you. Don't worry I won't do anything to you. Just please let me shoot this lion. The lion is trying to climb up the tree but keeps on falling down. That lion must be frustrated, no the lion is smart and will eventually get the carcass out of the tree.

No, I don't, that's what you say now. Listen you need to calm down and not let your feelings get out of control. I wasn't letting my feelings get out of control. I had enough arguing with you, the lion has what looks like a hole in his left side behind his shoulder. I don't know how the lion is still living after that.

        "Do you think that the lion is a zombie?"

        "No"

        "Have you ever heard of zombies otherwise?"

        "Yes"

        "What's a zombie lion?"

        "The lion is dead and is still living."

        "How can I believe such a crazy story?"

        "You should believe it, and don't doubt it."

        "So were looking at a zombie lion?"

"Yes," we most certainly are.

I wonder what made the lion sick

"Please let me shoot this crazy zombie lion?"

"No"

I don't want you to shoot the lion, why not the lion is dead and won't feel any pain while I'm shooting him. Take my rifle and please be gentle with it, I will.

If you knock the scope off of my rifle I'll be very angry with you. I don't lend my rifle out to everyone that I have met. I felt that you were a gentle, kind loving man. Look over there at the tree, the lion is now in the tree and I can see that blood is running out his mouth.

"Don't you see the blood running out from his mouth?"

"Yes," I do

I hope that my gun can kill the zombie lion, I hope that the disease that this lion has stopped with this lion, and doesn't spread onto more lions.

"How many bullets do you have with you?"

"I have six bullets with me."

"Is this rifle a single shot?"

"Yes"

You know this rifle has a lot of weight to it, and I like how it looks if you ever decide to sell your rifle let me know, I'll be sure to do that.

"Are you going to take a shot at the lion or not?"

"I'm going to take the shot when I'm good and ready."

You were ready to take the shot a few minutes ago, I know that but I need to wait for a better shot at him. The lion is facing away from me, so I have to wait for him to turn towards us. I could have took the shot by now.

"Would you stop bragging about how good of a shot you are and let me concentrate on the shot?"

"I'll let you go."

It's dark out here and it seems like the scope isn't illuminating correctly, that's because you don't have the scope turned on. There's a little button on the left side of the scope.

"It's a little black button, but you have to push it in with a lot of pressure."

"Did you get it?"

"Yes"

Thanks for the hint on where to turn it on at, I like the wooden stock

"How long have you had this rifle for?"

"I've had it for several years."

"Did you get this rifle from a gun shop?

"Yes," I did.

"Are you looking through the scope?"

"Yes"

The lion is still munching on the carcass, it looks like he's enjoying his meal.

"Has the lion turned around yet?"

"No"

I have to stand up, my legs are cramping up pretty bad. If you get up then you're going to put us in jeopardy of the lion spotting us. I don't care if the lion sees us, I'm going to take him out anyway.

"I'm being cautious and you're acting like a complete fool."

"Are you going to get up or take the shot?"

"I'm going to take a shot, instead of getting up."

"What made you change your mind so quickly?"

"I now realize that were in a tight situation."

"You just realized now that were in such dire straits?"

"Yes," I did

You're the most irresponsible hunter I've ever taken on a hunt. Thanks A lot, you didn't need to mention that last comment to me. I feel like you're disrespecting me.

I wanted to enjoy this hunt but now I'm no longer having any fun here. I want to go back to the safari truck and get out of Africa and never come back.

Remember you were the one who made up his mind to come to Africa to hunt in the first place. I just don't see this hunting trip getting any better for me. Then the lion let out a growl and looked back at them. The lion has turned towards us and now I can finally take the shot. Go ahead and pull the trigger and kill the zombie lion.

"For a hunter you aren't real good with guns"

"Are you out of practice?"

"No," and don't ever say that to me again

"Kansas pulled back the trigger and the bullet struck the lion between his eyes."

The lion immediately fell over on his left side. I got him, good shot, where did the bullet hit it. The bullet hit the lion right between his eyes. That was a good shot and it's probably better than I could have done.

"Aren't you happy that you were able to kill the zombie lion?"

"Yes"

I originally came here hoping that I could shoot a leopard.

"Aren't you going to take a look at the zombie lion?"

"No," and I don't care too.

I've heard just about enough from you, keep all of your comments to yourself now. If you don't mind I'm going to go look at the body of the dead zombie lion. Dakarai slowly walked towards the lion's body. The lion appeared to be shot two other times in the back.

The lion had blood all over his body, and there was a pool of blood under the lion's head. He bent down on his one knee and took a closer look at the lion's eyes. The lion's eyes were bright red and there was no pupil. This seemed very odd to him, Dakarai happened to look in the lion's mouth and it was missing some of his teeth.

Suddenly Dakarai heard something rustling around in a bush. The bush was seventy feet away from him, he was concerned about what may have been hiding in the bush. He quickly ran back to where Kansas was.

"What's the matter?"

"I heard something rustling around in a bush near me."

"What do you think it was?"

"I don't really know what it was."

"Could I please have my rifle back?"

"Yes," you can.

I'm going to reload the rifle because I'm afraid of what may lie inside the bush. You reload your rifle like a pro thank you for the compliment.

"Are those hollow point bullets or match grade?"

"They're match grade."

I have five bullets left, I'm ready to get in the safari truck and leave here.

"I'm not ready, why not?"

"I want to try to find you a leopard and who knows maybe there's a leopard inside the tall brown bush."

I sure hope you're right, it was so hot today, I'm glad it's dark out and is cooling down.

"How can you stand the high temperatures?"

"Over time I have gotten used to the high temperatures."

"Don't you get bad sunburns?"

"Yes," I do if I'm not careful.

I just heard a roar coming out of the bush, I think it could be a leopard, at least I hope it is. If it's not a leopard, I will want to end the hunt. Suddenly as Dakarai was watching the bush, a young leopard came walking out from behind the bush. Look over there, it's a leopard, I'm happy now.

"Would you mind letting me borrow your rifle again?"

"No," go right ahead

"I like how heavy this rifle is."

"Are you looking through the scope?"

"Yes," and I'm staring at the leopard.

"What's the leopard doing?"

"He's just standing by the dead zombie lions body."

"Does the leopard look good and healthy?"

"As far as I can see he is."

He must have been eating something and there was blood all over his mouth. But wait half of his tail looks like it has been bitten off and his left ear has a big hole through it. Something is definitely not right with this leopard.

"Are you still going to shoot the leopard?"

"Yes," but I'm afraid that he is infected with the same disease that the lion has.

"I thought you were so excited to see a leopard?"

"I was"

I'm afraid that most of the animals that are out there may be infected and are turning into the walking dead.

"Why must you be so negative?"

"It's true somehow these animals are spreading the virus around to each other."

"How do you know that it's a virus?"

"I don't know"

"How do you think they are going to stop the virus from spreading to any more animals?"

"That's a good question."

So you and I are going to have to go to the authorities and have this preserve shut down.

"What's that going to do?"

"It will keep the people safe and that's all what matters."

"How about the animals?"

"They're going to be on their own, only the strong animals will survive and the weak will perish."

Chapter: 4 Escape

I thought you would have a plan ready to get the animals away from one another so they can't infect each other. No, there are far too many animals on this preserve to separate all of them, it's just not possible.

Nothing is impossible, you're just trying to make up excuses so you won't have to get to work. No, that's not true, I'm a hard worker and aren't afraid of getting my hands dirty.

"Did all of your ancestors live in Africa?"

"Yes," and they all were great hunters of the savanna.

"So your great-grandfather lived in a cave?

"No," he lived in a small grass hut made from bushes and mud would hold everything together.

He would make a campfire in front of his hut to keep big cats away from his hut while he was sleeping. That was smart of him, I miss my grandfather tremendously.

"He was one of the legendary hunters."

"You mean to tell me that he was a legend?"

"Yes," he was

"Do you have any old black and white pictures of him?"

"No"

I own a camera, we have shops around here.

"Where did you get the rifle from?"

"A rebel group"

"Where are the rebels at?"

"They're about an hour's walk away from here."

"Are they friendly?"

As far as I know, they still are, you better find out if they're hostile or not. Suddenly headlights were coming upon them

"Who's that?"

"I don't know, look the driver of that truck is letting the truck get out of control, we better watch ourselves."

No, were okay but the driver of that truck is about to crash into and run over the poor leopard.

"I wonder why he's driving towards the leopard?"

"Maybe he's planning on running him over."

He just crashed directly into the leopard. That poor leopard that you wanted to shoot is dead. Hold on I'm going to go find out why this man just ran over the leopard. Hey, Sir?

"What?"

"Why are you on this game preserve?"

In case you don't know I actually work here, and what's happening here isn't right. I've never saw the animals on this preserve act so crazy. The animals die and somehow keep on walking around here. It's really beginning to freak me out.

"What's your name Sir?"

"My name is Faraji, and I've been working on this preserve for 2 years."

"Why did you run over the leopard-like that?"

"It's the only way I've been able to kill the animals."

The Leopard that you just ran over is trying to get up. I don't think the leopard will be able to get out from beneath the front tire of this heavy truck.

I have an American hunter with me and his name is Kansas and he's waited all day and half the evening for a leopard and you run over the only leopard that he was going to shoot.

If he wants he can just have the leopards dead body. No, he wants a healthy leopard that he can shoot. I'm sorry bud but there aren't any more alive healthy animals in this game preserve. These zombie animals have so far killed four people who work here.

"How do you know that?"

"I witnessed it"

"You did nothing to stop the attacking zombie animals?"

"I shot at them and I hit them, but they wouldn't stop attacking the people."

"Did the other people have guns on them?"

"No"

They didn't know that they were going to get attacked. I felt so bad for them, I felt like I had let them down.

"Do you think that the dead people may come back to life?"

"No," this virus is just in the animals.

"How many of the lions on this preserve are infected with the virus?"

"Sadly, all of them are."

That's just not okay with me. Yes, but that's how it is and it cannot be changed unless you go back in time and we can't do that. Look the leopard is still trying to get up.

"Why don't you finish off the leopard?"

"I don't have my rifle with me, I lend it to the American hunter."

Get the rifle back from him and shoot this poor leopard he is dead and is suffering.

"Could I have my rifle back?"

"Yes," sure, take it.

Dakarai took his rifle and ran over to leopard and at close range shot the leopard right between the eyes. The leopard fell over and never got up again. Good shot, thank you.

"Have you been running over all the animals on the preserve?"

"No," just this leopard.

"Are there more lions walking around here?"

"Yes," as far as I know.

"Are the few elephants that are on preserve sick too?"

"No," the virus didn't get to them yet.

"How about the giraffes?"

"No," they seem normal.

"How could that be?"

"I have no idea."

Dakarai you and me and Kansas are in grave danger and we need to think about getting out of here real soon, or we may end up dead like the other people.

"How did the lions and other animals get after the other workers?"

"One of the workers had left the door wide open and "the Lions got inside of the office building.

"Did the Lions make a mess of the office?"

"Yes"

They tore it all up and killed all the workers, by the time I had got to the office, the front door was wide open and paperwork was scattered all over the floor. The wind blew some of the papers around outside of the office. The office was a real mess, there was blood all over the floor of the office.

Some of the workers were missing their arms and legs, I mean it was such a horrific scene. It was so bad that I had got sick to my stomach. I ended up throwing up all over the place.

"Do you know if any of the primates on the preserve have been infected?"

"No," not that I know of

"How about the hippos?"

"Yes," they are infected and are running around here, I actually saw a zombie hippo on my way over here.

"Why did you come over here?"

"On this particular part of the preserve is where the zebras are and I was going to check on them."

I would feel a lot better if the both of you got in my truck with me. We will then. I'm going to close up all the windows and we need to get going. Here comes a hippo.

The hippo is now directly behind us, so you will have to go forward to get out of here. Get this truck in gear and let's go. I'll just hold on; we don't have the time to hold on. If that hippo gets any closer to us, then he'll be on top of this truck.

"Did you say that the hunter wanted the body of the leopard?"

"No," I don't need the leopard's body.

Let's just get ourselves out of here. Step on it. What do you think I'm doing, this truck is no sports car, this truck is old and moves slow

"How fast are we going now?"

"I don't know the speedometer broke yesterday."

"How did it break?"

"I surely didn't break it, this truck is old and falling apart."

"Does this truck have a full tank of gas?"

"Yes," it does, oh thank goodness.

"Where are you driving to?"

"I'm driving to the main gate so that we can get out of here."

"Isn't there something that we can do to stop all of the zombie animals?"

"No," unless you want to die fighting them off.

"How do you know that were going to die fighting the zombie animals?"

"There's no way to kill them, that's not true."

"How do you know that?"

"Usually to kill a zombie you would shoot them in between the eyes."

I've heard of that, but there are hundreds of animals on this preserve, and there are a few zombie lions left.

"How are you going to fight off three lions at one time with just one rifle?"

"With one bullet at a time."

Speed up, it's taking us forever to get to where we need to be.

"Are we almost at the front gate?"

Yes, just a short ways now.

You're a good driver but I'm worried we aren't going to get out of here alive with these zombie animals running all around. All three of us are going to get out of here alive I promise.

"What are you doing?"

"I got out to try to open the main gate, but it's jammed and won't open."

"Would you help me?"

"Yes," I will

"What do you want me to do?"

"I want you to come over by me and help me push the gate."

"Are you ready to push on the gate?"

"Yes"

Now push, I am but it's not budging. Hold on lets both push one more time and the gate should open. Now push, oh thank goodness, the gate is moving.

Quickly push the gate open. I did, just give me a moment to get in the truck and pull it forward. Faraji pulled out the truck in gear and quickly pulled forward past the gate. Dakarai closed the gate back up.

With one push, he was able to close the gate. Were now home free, see that guys I knew we were going to get out of there alive. The animals are now stuck in the preserve.

"That's what he wants."

"How come you aren't saying much?"

"I just don't have anything to say at this moment in time."

"Aren't you happy we were able to escape the preserve?"

"Yes"

"I feel bad for all the animals who aren't sick who are going to become sick once the sick animals attack them."

"Do you want to go home now?"

"No"

I would rather spend time with you guys, there's a lion up against the fence trying to get out of the preserve. He appears to be infected with the virus.

"Do you think we should take the lion out of its misery?"

"No," I think we should let the zombie lion alone.

"What do you think?"

"I think that we should take the lion out of its misery."

The both of us believe that we shouldn't kill the lion and you are the only one thinks we should kill the lion. So, we aren't going to kill the lion. No, I'm not, it's just the way you think I am. You don't know me that well, let's look past our differences and have a meaningful conversation together.

"Are you going to back to the United States soon?"

"Yes," I am and why are you asking me that?

"I was just curious."

"What's the matter?"

"I'm tired replied Kansas and want to go home and be with my family."

I'm going to pull out my laptop when we get back to the lodge and buy a plane ticket and fly home today.

"Are we almost back to the lodge?"

"Yes," in 10 minutes.

I'm worried that the zombie lions are going to break down the fence. No that's not going to happen.

"How do you know?"

"I just know."

Chapter 5: In Jeopardy

I would be so surprised if a zombie lion knocked down the fence. The fence around the preserve has been up for more than twenty years and no lion or elephants have knocked down the fence. The fence has barbed wire over the top of it and the fence is also electrified to keep the elephants from smashing down the fence.

"Does that answer your questions about the fence?"

"I didn't have any questions about what kind of fence it was."

Would you stop arguing with the hunter, I'm developing a bad headache. Just please be quiet the both of you. We have arrived at the lodge. Dakarai jumped out of the truck and ran into the lodge. He swung open the door and left himself in, while it took some time for Faraji and Kansas to get out of the truck.

Let's just go inside, once in the lodge Kansas sat down at a table and pulled out his laptop from his briefcase. Dakarai and I are going to go relax in the lounge room. If you need anything let us know, I'll surely do that.

"Did you feel the ground shake?"

"No"

I know what I felt and wasn't making things up. Just take a look outside, I will just to make to you happy, Dakarai slowly walked out the front door and immediately came running back in.

You won't believe what I saw, there's a huge bull elephant standing just yards away from the lodge, he came charging when I went to go outside. So, brace for impact, the huge bull elephant slammed into the front door and knocked the doors inward. Watch out, get out of the way.

"Where's your rifle?"

"It's here beside me"

I'm going to take down the elephant by myself, the bull elephant soon gave up on smashing the lodge and walked a few yards away. He's a rogue bull elephant and needs to be stopped. So, take the shot and stop talking. Dakarai walked out the front entrance and precisely aimed his rifle and fired.

The bullet struck the elephant in the head, it slumped over and collapsed down onto its side and remained there motionless. The loud blast disturbed Faraji and he came running out into the lobby.

"What's going on?"

"Dakarai had to shoot a bull elephant because it was smashing into the lodge and causing damage."

You should have told me that you guys needed help and I would have come out and helped you guys.

"Are you done shooting?"

"Yes"

Good then I will talk to you both later. Bye now, Soon afterwards Dakarai and Kansas settled down and they both fell asleep while sitting on the couch. A loud growl nearby woke both men up, they both jumped up. I don't wanna know what just made that growl, we're probably going to find out soon.

There better be a bullet in the chamber of your gun, there is. You better hope that there's not more than one creature running around out there. They heard some ruckus going on in the other room, since you're the hunter I'll let you go after it. Kansas peaked around the corner, and saw the creature.

It was a leopard, and it was missing one of its legs. Blood was dripping out of its mouth and eyes. Instead of coming towards him, it was going the opposite way. It crawled along the floor, leaving drops of blood behind. Once it crawled outside something much larger came and grabbed it.

This left him in shock, he stayed still and didn't make a move. Then the creature came walking inside, that's when he saw that it was a lion. The lion came closer to him, and he fired hitting it in the head and it collapsed. Dakarai came running into the room, and saw that the lion was laying down. I heard the gun go off and had to come out and check, you and I are no longer safe here.

There's no way that we could defend against a few of these lions, there's a bunker under this building. I suggest that we go down there after we're done talking, let's just go now.

They walked into the backroom, and opened the door that went down to the bunker. They entered the bunker, and walked down a few steps. Dakarai flicked the light switch and the lights came on, I think that we should stay down here for at least 2 or 3 days.

If I remember correctly there should be a puzzle in a box that we can put together, and we can do some sand art. There's plenty of water down here so don't be shy to drink it. There's someone knocking on the door of the bunker, I'm wondering who that could be.

Hopefully it's a rescuer, they shouted come in. The man came walking down the steps, hello fellas. I'm part of a rescue team, we're glad to see you. Come with me and let's get out of here, they walked out of the building and got into the truck and took off.

One hour later they came to a small airport, and got on a plane that was headed to Texas. Once back in Texas, both men took it easy at Dakarai's home. Meanwhile in Michigan there was a man named Grayson who was a nice man in his early thirties and his dad Isaiah is the town's mayor. Grayson has five good friends that he likes to spend time with. His dad Isaiah is a hard worker and doesn't like to take vacations. It's been three years since his last vacation, he took his son along with him to the Cayman islands. They spent a week there and both got a good tan, he has a girlfriend but she doesn't want to get married yet. But instead got engaged to her, Grayson and Isaiah have always gotten along well with each other; Grayson likes to spend a lot of time outside.

They live in a nice quite little town, the temperature in the summertime is nice. The winters are very harsh and Isaiah is getting tired of shoveling snow, last year they got four inches of snow and a layer of black ice.

Isaiah's car had some ice stuck on the wind shield, he had to work up a sweat just to get the ice off. Isiah's son helped to get all the snow off of his car's hood, Isaiah drives a rolls Royce town car. His favorite color is blue, so he had his car painted blue. The paint job was rather expensive but he didn't care.

It took the painters 2 hours to paint his car blue. He even had them put a blue light beneath the car to make it look like it was lit up all of the time. He loves to listen to classical music, his favorite composer is Bach.

He had a large sound system installed in his car, so when he turns up his music it makes the car rumble. His son doesn't like to ride along with him, he says that it makes him feel embarrassed. His son couldn't afford a car as nice as his, he had a nice puddle jumper. It was a foreign model from Austria. It does get good gas mileage, a lot better than what his dad's car gets. Grayson doesn't like to drive his car on the highway. Because last year he was in a bad accident and got bad whiplash in his neck. Sometimes when it rains he neck aches. He had a nice Beatle bug. But it was destroyed in the accident. He wasn't even going too fast; he was doing the speed limit.

The other driver was going sixty-five miles per hour, and hit him right in the back. The impact caused his back bumper to come completely off and the exhaust pipe fell off. The other car was an old kit car.

It kind of resembled a cobra. He was just a young kid. He was twenty-two years old, and had rich parents who would buy him anything that he wanted. Grayson wasn't jealous though.

He filed a claim through his car insurance company. The car insurance company had helped him by giving him a deductible towards his next car. Although he doesn't remember how much he had to pay out of pocket for his next car. Grayson works as an appraiser for a good 5-star company.

His boss is a very patient man who gives his workers a change to go on his health insurance plan. He gives out bonuses to the appraiser who does the best work, So far Grayson has won 2 awards.

The first award was for he came to work on time for 3 straight years, then the second award was for appraising 4 houses in 1 day. His boss was ecstatic and told him that he could have the next day off with pay.

Grayson prefers to always dress professionally. He wears a nice black suit with a blue tie. He ties his tie nicely every day, and when he gets home he takes the tie off and puts it away in his dresser drawer. All his clothes have to be put away folded and ironed.

He does the ironing by hand and won't let anyone else to fold or to iron his clothes. He's currently single, but in the past 2 months he has been talking to a nice young lady who he met when he was doing an appraisal a month prior. The women's name is Kathleen. She has a kind loving personality, and loves to give people hugs.

She gave Grayson two hugs while he was trying to appraise her house, and likes to watch scary movies about zombies and also likes to watch dramas. When Grayson came to her front door to appraise her house her cat had gotten out of her house and tried to jump up on Grayson.

Grayson backed up and the cat walked over by his side and walked in
between his legs. He said come on, please come out here and get your
cat. So she came out and grabbed her cat and held him in her skinny
arms.

"How long is it going to take you to appraise my
house?"

"Typically small homes take me half an hour, but it all
depends on the size of the house"

"Why so long?"

"I have to go in every room and measure it and sketch
it"

"I have to look around in the attic, I have to look for
any damages that maybe in your house."

"Like what kind of damages?"

"Water damage, smoke damage, and any other kind of
damages."

"Am I going to have to pay for damages in my house?"

"Yes," you will.

"What's wrong?"

"I'm just thinking about what I have to do today."

"Can I come in?"

"Yes," but be careful my two sons like to leave Legos and stuffed animals in every room of the house.

"I'm always tripping over them and I don't want you to fall."

"How old are your sons?"

"They're 2 and 4 years old."

"Are they good kids?"

"They're good most of the time, but I'm always disciplining them."

"Do you hit them hard?"

"No," of course not, they're smart kids and I just have to raise my voice and then they're good.

"Do you just have 1 cat?"

"I used to have 2 cats, but my other cat Oliver died just last week."

You have a nice house here, the only problem is, it smells like cat pee in the living room and dining room.

"Do you ever let the cats out in your back yard?"

"Yes," I do

"Why?"

"I just wanted to know that to know if they were peeing the house."

"Have you ever caught them peeing in the house?"

"No," I haven't

"Why do you have to ask so many questions to ask me about my cats?"

"These are just questions that I ask everyone who owns cats."

"I don't really trust you in my house, so please don't take too long in here."

"Are you threatening me?"

"No," I just don't like strangers walking around my house.

Remember I called you early this morning and reminded you that I was coming over, that's true I really shouldn't be complaining.

"Where are your kids?"

"They're at my grandma's house."

They have been at there grandma's house for the past 3 days.

"Then why aren't there toys cleaned up and nicely put away?"

"I just haven't had a moment to do that yet."

"I made some extra oatmeal this morning"

"Would you like some?"

"No," thanks I ate breakfast already

"Do you ever clean the top of the stove?"

"No," I couldn't live that way.

"Why not?"

"You need to keep your kitchen clean or it will draw bugs and could even cause you to get sick."

I'm not worried about getting sick, I hope that after you cook this evening you take some time and wipe off the stove top. You're not my dad or mother, so let it go.

I will then I'm sorry for saying anything to you, that's a nice rug that you have in your kitchen. I got that rug from my grandma who had it at her house, the carpet in the living room looks relatively new.

"How long ago did you have it put in?"

"I had it put in when I moved in here three months ago."

You have good taste when it comes to carpeting, thanks that was a nice compliment. I think brown carpet looks good in here, I thought the same way.

"How comes there's a small hole in the wall?"

"One day I was feeling angry and threw a book at one of my cats and well it hit the wall."

My one cat pooped on the floor right in front of me while I was sitting on my couch. You know what this couch in the living room looks terrible, there are a few rips in the fabric.

"How long have you had the couch for?"

"I've had this couch for way too long."

"I should of threw it out three years ago."

"Do you let the cats up on your couch?"

"Yes," I do, is that a bad thing?

"No," but that's why your couch is so ripped up.

"It seems to me that you let these cats go wherever they want in the house."

"I don't like cats at all, I think they are stinky and they don't act very smart."

"So you're a dog person?"

"Yes," I am, okay enough talk it's time for you to get a move on.

"Why are you being so pushy?"

"Are you hiding something?"

"I can tell that you do."

"Are you going to tell me or am I going to have to keep asking you?"

"No," I have a zombie in a cage in my bedroom

"What?"

"That's the weirdest thing I've heard all day."

"Is it really alive?"

"Yes," he's very much alive.

"What do you feed him?"

"I feed him raw chicken legs and steak."

"It sounds like he eats good."

"Does it cost a lot to keep on feeding him?"

"Yes it does."

"What happens if you don't feed him?"

"Then he growls, and shakes the cage."

"Does he sleep or is he always awake?"

"Yes," He sleeps during the day, if I'm not in the room with him.

"Did you give him a name?"

"Yes," I call him Chris

"Where did you find him?"

"That's a long story and I don't really want to tell you the story."

"How old is the zombie?"

"He told me that he's 38"

He always has a puzzled look on his face, maybe he's a confused zombie. His one eye is green and the other one's brown. He's pretty tall, why don't you come with me into the bedroom and take a look at him. The smell coming from your bedroom almost knocked me over, It smells like rotting flesh and nachos.

"Does the zombie like to eat chips?"

"Yes," sometimes when he behaves himself I throw a bag of nachos into his cage, he thanks me for the chips

"Does he eat the bag and the chips? Or just the chips."

"He's so goofy that he eats the bag and the chips."

"After he's done eating the bag he stares at me and has a smirk on his face.

Chapter 6: Wasting Time

I'm surprised that he doesn't get sick from eating the chip bag, he looks just horrible, there are so many rips in his shirt and pants. He even has blood running down his face which is coming out of his mouth. His teeth look like they are all rotten and are about to fall out. He really stinks and is stinking up your house.

"Are you going to tell your boss about my zombie living in my house?"

"No," I'm not going to say a word.

"Have you ever tried to teach him how to brush his teeth?"

"No"

"Why would I do that?"

"He's not smart at all"

One time my cat caught a mouse, and I threw the dead mouse in Chris's cage and he grabbed the mouse and ate it right away, I don't even think he chewed up the mouse. It was so disgusting that I threw up all over the carpet in my bedroom.

"Does he stand up all day?"

"No," he sits down, like he's doing now.

"I can't stand hearing the rap music in this room"

"Could you please turn it down?"

Chris likes to listen to rap music he seems to make him calm, I don't care please turn it down or off.

"It's off now"

"Is that better?"

"Much better"

"I didn't know that zombies liked rap music, he does though it makes him chill out."

"What if you wouldn't turn the music back on?"

"He'll shake the cage violently and growl and moan.

"What do your kids think about him?"

"They think that he's cool and they think it's funny when he gets mad and growls at me."

"Does your grandma know about him?"

"Yes," and she wants me to get rid of him.

She told me 3 times to get rid of him, but I don't want to let him go. But it's not fair to him.

I know that, now I don't want you to be in my house much longer. Let me finish up going through your house.

"Is Chris afraid of bugs?"

"No," he actually likes to eat stink bugs.

One day 2 stink bugs were crawling on his shirt and he caught them and ate them both before they could fly away. He laughed afterwards, and burped.

"So he's quick?"

"Yes,"

I get lonely most of the time. That's the true reason why he's here. Sometimes he'll tell me a funny joke.

"Does he like to eat a lot?"

"Yes"

I'm running out of food so I had to give him so green moldy bread. Did he eat it all, and he let out a burp? I didn't know that a zombie could burp.

"Has he ever escaped?"

"No"

It looks like those chains around him are too tight, no they're just fine. I couldn't imagine sleeping with such an ugly creature.

"Do you keep one open at night?"

"No," I sleep just fine and he sleeps good too.

He actually snores when he's sleeping, that's so funny, I've never heard of a zombie snoring before. This zombie snores every night. That must be annoying, no after a while you get used to it. I don't want you to go up into the attic. I see that you have a hula hoop, and he went over to the cage and began quickly undoing the chains.

Kathleen came running over, stop what you're doing. Chris came out of the cage, and Grayson handed him the hula hoop and he began to dance around with it. You see Chris isn't going to hurt you, you were worrying for nothing.

Now he can help me to clean the house, and Chris moped. Chris wandered into the hallway, and was heading to the kitchen. If I were you, you better go see what he's doing in there. They both walked into the kitchen and Chris was sitting at the kitchen table. Chris said I want some tarts, don't worry I'll get you some.

"Did you mean pop tarts?"

"Yes"

Kathleen opened up the cabinet and brought out a box of pop tarts, and put the box in front of Chris. He opened the box and took out 2 pop tarts and immediately ate them.

I think that I'm going to take a look around your attic anyway. You have been warned though, I don't care, it can't be that bad.

"You have to find out for yourself don't you?"

"Yes," I do. I still can't believe that you have a zombie living in your house.

I wasn't going to mention this but my cousin's a trash man, alright well that was random. He looks for road kill for me, and I give it to the Chris to eat. I don't think that's legal, I know that's why I didn't want to mention it. Please don't tell the police about it, I won't and I won't tell them that you have a zombie living in your bedroom.

"Have you told anyone else about the zombie?"

"No," I haven't.

I think that if you don't want to clean your house then you should have a cleaning lady come once a week. No, I'm not going to spend the money for that.

I'm sure that you must have some extra money laying around. No, I don't and it's none of your business how much money I make or don't make.

"Is that understand?"

"Yes," it is.

"Could you please move out of my way so that I can go up into the attic?"

"Yes," I will

but please be careful climbing up the steps, listen I have climbed up worse looking steps then these. Grayson put his head up to look around in the attic and spider web got in his left eye and another up his nose. He sneezed but kept on looking around.

There were three card board boxes with stuff overflowing out of them. There were old magazines and old lamps and blankets in the one box. He climbed up all the way into the attic.

He was too tall to stand up in the attic, so he stayed slouched over. He looked in the second box and there was a whole roll of paper towels and an old wood burning kit. The wood burning kit wasn't even open, and had a layer of dust on it.

He looked over at the far corner of the room and saw what he thought was something hanging up, he went to walk over, and all of a sudden it flapped. Then he realized that it was a bat, he wasn't afraid of the bat. There were spider webs around the bat, but the bat didn't mind it. Then a spider came crawling over towards him.

He didn't care, another spider came down from the ceiling and crawled down on his right shoulder. It was a little wolf spider, it was all brown and crawled along quickly, it crawled down his neck and he caught the spider and squished it between his fingers. He saw some more spider's webs in the left hand corner of the attic. The bat remained in the corner and kept on flapping its wings.

Then the bat fell down onto the floor of the attic and began to fly around the attic. It flew into some large spider webs. The spider webs were now all over him, He seemed to be confused and kept on flying in a circle towards him.

He that there was a little brown broom just below where the bat was flying. He thought to himself if I reach for this broom, is the bat going to swoop down and bite me. He thought on oh well it's not worth getting bit by the bat.

He was going to sweep up the attic but then decided not to, It was so hot in the attic that it made him sweat and he couldn't stand it. Then two stink bugs flew into the bat, the bat reacted and flew overhead of him again. He grew tired of the bat flying overhead. So he opened the latch to get out of the attic, he carefully climbed down the ladder, but didn't see Kathleen.

His head was really itchy from the spider web being on it, he used his right hand brushed off his head. He felt his around his shirt and there was a stink bug crawling down his back. He left the stink bug there and brushed off his nice dress pants and went on through the house.

He heard a loud growl and thought to himself I hope that the zombie didn't escape. Suddenly Kathleen came running into the room, she had a nervous look on her face and was shaking.

"What's the matter with you?"

"I walked into my bedroom and oh my Chris caught my cat and tried to take him into the cage and eat him."

"Were you able to stop him?"

"No," he took him in the cage with him and killed my last cat.

"What's he doing now?"

"He's eating my cat"

"Why didn't you stop him?"

"He's too strong and I didn't get there in time."

"I'm sorry about your cat"

"Are you going to get another cat?"

"No," I'm not; this was the last one.

"Why didn't you scream at Chris?"

Chris doesn't like it, then he gets more violent. You're taking a great risk just letting the zombie live in your house. I know but the zombie entertains us, we'll that's not right.

"Do you have cable?"

"Yes," we have cable and 2 televisions.

"Didn't you see the flat screen television on the bedroom wall?"

"No," I didn't.

I was too focused on the zombie.

"What do you do when your friends come over?"

"I keep them in my living room, and don't let them in my bedroom."

"Do they ever ask you why they can't go in your bedroom."

"No," they don't and that's a good thing.

"I do like to talk a lot."

"Do your kids ever play near Chris?"

"No," I would never do that, he might reach his arms out of the cage and grab them.

He just killed my cat and now I'm not going to go near him. You know he really stinks like rotting flesh, and there was some large black garbage flies buzzing around him.

"He just keeps on moaning and groaning and it's really getting on my nerves, maybe that means he's done eating.

I'm no zombie whisper or shrink but I will do my best to help you. Listen you grumpy silly stinky zombie, you need to calm down and relax. Because if you don't we are going to kick you out of here.

"Did you hear me Chris?"

"Yes"

Grayson it seems like, you have made him very angry.

"Could you try to say something else to him?"

"Yes I will"

"He shook his head and said no"

You aren't doing what I asked you to do.

"Why don't you turn the rap music back on?"

"Because he doesn't need the music on all of the time."

"I don't care just turn it back on."

"Can I go back to work now?"

"Yes, but, you didn't make Chris calm down.

"I don't care about that stinky gross zombie."

"Can you please lead me to the basement and let me measure it?"

"Sure thing, thank you for helping me."

As they both were walking down the hallway, Grayson bumped the wall and accidentally knocked over a picture. Hey that was a nice picture of my grandfather that you knocked over. I didn't knock it off of the wall purposely.

"Is there anything that I should worry about when going into the basement?"

"No," there shouldn't be anything down there.

"Has it rained around here lately?"

"Yes," it has, and there was bad lightning storm here last night.

"If the power goes out do you have a backup generator?"

"No," I don't and I don't want to buy one either.

"You're really against that."

Kathleen slowly opened the basement door, oh wow these are really rickety steep basement steps. I know they are and I don't like to walk down them that much.

There's a big problem, what's that, I can tell that were basement is flooded. Water has come up to the first step, and I won't walk waist deep into the basement.

"I will though that's fine with me."

"Could you hand me a flash light?"

"It's right here by the basement door, okay I see it now"

"Why are you walking in the water in the basement?"

"I just want to see what's left in the basement."

Alright thank you for gently handing me the flash light. You're welcome, now be careful and don't hurt yourself. I'm an adult I think I can handle myself.

"Why are you splashing around down there like a fish?"

"I wasn't trying to."

"What did you have in your basement before?"

"I just had an old dining room table in the basement and that's all?"

"Yes," that's all.

My basement was never completed and I don't care to fix up the basement.

"You have really set your ways, haven't you?"

"Yes," I have

This water down in the basement is so cold, I don't know how much longer I'm going to be done here for. You know that water in the basement has a bad smell to it. It smells like old rotten eggs that have been sitting around for a month.

"How can you stand the cold stinky basement water?"

"I don't know because I'm holding my nose with my right hand and the flashlight with my left hand."

"What happened?"

"I just tripped over the last step in the basement and the cold water made my hair all wet. I want you to think about getting out of the basement."

"Why?"

"You could get a cold from being in the cold stinky water so long."

Stop talking like a Dr, I know my body pretty well, I'm just looking out for you.

"I'm a kind guy and like to be nice."

"Would you like me to be mean to you?"

"No," I wouldn't.

"Now what?"

"I hit my knee on the table in the basement."

I want you to get out of there now. Alright I will, now I'm going to have to take a shower.

"What's wrong with that?"

"The water heater hasn't worked for a month and I'm tired of taking cold showers."

"Why do you like to let yourself and this house suffer for so long?"

"I don't know probably because I'm so lazy and don't want anyone coming into my house."

I have gotten used to taking cold showers, and I don't spend but ten minutes in the shower.

"Are you coming up the steps or am I going to have to go down there and pull you out?"

"No," I'm coming, I just had to find the steps.

"I'm coming up and don't worry I'm okay."

"How comes you are shivering?"

I'm cold and of course I will get much colder after I take another cold shower. I'm worried about Chris, don't worry about him. Worry about yourself more. I'll try, but he's still hungry and don't anything left to feed him and he's going to be angry at me tonight and keep me up all night.

"Do you have a roll of duct tape somewhere in this house?"

Yes," I do

"Would you think about using it on Chris?"

"No," I would never get that close to him.

"You're funny"

"Why?"

"Nothing seems to bother you. Your whole house is falling apart all around you and you don't seem to care."

"What kind of condition is your roof in?"

"It's not so bad, there's one leak in the roof in the living room, that's bad enough don't you think?"

"No," I don't think so.

Chapter 7: Lost In Conversation

This house is in bad condition and suggest that you either get this house repaired or move out. This house is falling apart like the rotting body of the zombie.

Soon you're going to get sick from living near a zombie, I hope that you don't turn into a zombie. Don't worry, I'm not going to get that close to him. What if he reaches his arms out of the cage, and pulls you closer to him and he bites you. It's never going to happen. That's what you think, now if you would excuse me and let me go take a shower.

"Can I go back into your backyard now?"

"You can but be careful my backyard is a muddy mess."

I'm not worried about a little mud and dirt. I will be out soon, alright then, Grayson walked out the back door and walked into the small fenced in back yard.

There was some grass growing, but it was all dead and the rest of the yard was full of mud. The gray fence has a large crack in it. The spouting was barely hanging on, and looked like if a good wind blew it would fall down.

The one window by the back door was so full of dust and cob webs. That you couldn't even see in the window itself. The window must have not been cleaned for years.

There were five dead stink bugs laying toes up in the window sill. By the very edge of the property was one daisy growing, the sun felt hot as it was beading down on his forehead.

He thought wow today is going to be hot. He thought to himself why don't I just write down that this house has to be bulldozed and have it rebuilt. He thought on and a he heard a loud screech from a crow that had landed on the fence beside him.

You silly bird, you're screeching is giving me a migraine. Now stop it. Just then Kathleen came walking out into the backyard. That didn't take you long, No, it was another cold shower, and the sun's making feel warm once again.

"Did you check on Chris again?"

"No," I didn't and I don't want to either.

Just then a jet passed over head and spooked him

"Do planes usually pass by your house?"

"Yes," they do and I'm used to it now.

"You aren't afraid of much are you?"

"No," I'm not and I'm not afraid of a zombie.

I would never let a zombie be with me in my bedroom, I know that Grayson you just got done saying that.

"Do you have any more questions about my house Grayson?"

"Yes," I do, in fact, do you not like to clean windows?

"Yes"

I don't like to clean at all or the least possible, you know you have a lot to learn about life. I know that, and I don't care. You're proving to me how stubborn you are. I realize that.

"What's your question about the house?"

"How long has this fence been back here for?"

It's been back here for going on three months,

"Who helped you to put it up?"

"A friend of mine"

"Why?

"He did a lousy job on it"

it's a wooden fence and is beginning to fall apart.

"Do you see this large crack in the wood?"

"Yes," I do

Soon this fence is going to deteriorate and fall down and then you will get a fine.

"How do you know I'm going to get a fine?"

"It's just what I'm told, by my boss."

You seem to know a lot about appraising, thank you.

"Do you know what kind of wood the fence is made out of?"

"No," I don't know about wood

"Do you?"

"Yes," I do, of course you do.

"What don't you know about?"

"I don't know much about zombies and he chuckled.

You can learn from my zombie, I don't want to learn any more about your zombie. I'm sure you do though, you seem so serious all of the time.

"Why's that?"

"I have a job to do here and don't want to laugh or smile right now."

You're a serious man most of the time I can tell, I can't stand how muddy this yard is. My nice dress shoes are probably going to get ruined. Don't say that, it's the truth. Mud isn't good for any shoe.

"Why didn't you put on a pair of boots, to come here?"

"I have to look presentable and not like a mountain man."

"You won't look bad in boots"

"How do you know?"

"I Just know."

"Do you like to make up stories?"

"No," I do tell the truth most of the time, you're
talking like a politician.

Thanks for that comment, you didn't need to say that out loud, some
comments you need to keep to yourself.

"Do you vote?"

"I do and I don't always like to talk about politics while
I'm doing my job."

"What's that thing strapped to your left side?"

"It's a laser measuring device."

I thought it was a cell phone, no it's not good to have a cell phone
strapped to your side.

"Why not?"

"Because the cell phone releases invisible rays of
radiation that disrupts your bodies nervous system.

You know I have never heard of that before, it sounds so silly to me."

"You will learn a lot from me."

"Where's your cell phone?"

"It's in my car"

"Why?"

"I was just curious"

"How comes most of the grass in your backyard is either dead or is turning yellow?"

"I don't know and I don't really care."

How's your front yard?

"It's doing good"

"There's a lot of grass growing in the front yard."

"Did you plant any grass in your front yard?"

"No"

It was already growing when I moved in, for not caring about your yard, you keep it looking all trimmed up and nice.

"How big's your garage?"

"It's a two car garage and trust me you don't want to look inside."

"Why not?"

"I have so much junk in it."

"Why don't you have a garage sale tomorrow?"

"No," I don't plan on selling certain things.

"Like what certain things?"

"Like the bicycle that I had since I was nine years old and the one Barbie doll that I didn't take out of the box yet."

I don't think that doll is worth very much anyway.

"How do you know that?"

"I don't know I'm just guessing."

"Have you ever sold anything that ment something special to you?"

"No," I haven't

I don't have anything that means much to me in my house.

"Can I ask you something?"

"Sure go ahead"

"Are you single or what?"

"Yes," I'm single and no I'm not looking for a girlfriend.

"Do you know what kind it is?"

"No," I don't

I've had this camera for 2 years and it works great for appraising. For my job I have to take a lot of pictures and this particular camera has a large memory card that can hold hundreds of pictures. I thought that you would have used your cell phones camera to take all the pictures of my house.

"Did you take a picture of Chris?"

"No"

I have not taken a picture of your bedroom yet. I was going to do that last. You were in the room and you had a chance to take the picture but didn't. You know the garage doors white paint is peeling off.

I know that it's peeling, but I can't find the right white paint to paint it with. What a shallow excuse, you must be the laziest person I have met. Stop it, I'm not.

"Would you like to go on a date with me tonight?"

"No," thanks, I don't know you well enough and a date is too soon.

"Are you afraid to date or something?"

"No," I'm not and when I'm ready I will date someone.

It seems like all women want to do is go on dates and spend all their money shopping. Yes, that's true, and I do like to shop till I drop.

"Are you a smoker?"

"Yes," indeed I am

"What's your favorite kind of cigarette?"

"I don't have a favorite brand."

I smoke whatever kind. Just to let you know I don't like the smell of cigarettes, I think they make a person stink. I don't think I stink, I make sure to put on my deodorant every morning. I do take a shower every morning, so it can't be that bad. At least your nails aren't yellow like Chris's nails are.

"How comes you let your hair down, it makes you look messy?"

"I don't think it makes my face look messy, but I will put them in a bun if you want."

"Would that make you happy?"

"Yes," then just ask me to put my hair up in a bun and I will.

"Does the garage door still function and open?"

"No," the motor in the garage door stopped working, last week.

"You didn't want to get it replaced?"

"No," it's not something important to me.

It should be, this is your house and you should want to take good care of it. After I leave here 2 men are going to show up and help you to fix up this run down house.

"Why?"

"I have 2 guy friends who redue houses for a living and the one is an interior decorator."

I don't need my house redecorated it's fine the way it is, that's what you think, but I think otherwise. I can't believe that your kids are living in this house.

"Haven't they gotten sick from the mold from the basement?"

"No," they stay very healthy.

"Do they eat all their vegetables at dinner time?

"Yes," they do, now please get on with taking pictures of the garage.

"Are you trying to rush me out of here?"

"Yes," I am

You need to learn how to wait then, since the garage door motor stopped working.

"How am I going to open the door?"

"Just hold on and I will push on the door at the same time that you do and I'm sure that the door will slide right up."

That's wishful thinking, I hope your idea works. We're pushing, and this door isn't going anywhere. Let's try one more time, I'm going to do it again. I'm already getting very hot and don't want to sweat anymore. Would you stop being lazy, I'm not a lazy guy though. I don't care.

Work is work and you don't seem like a hard worker to me, you don't know me that well yet. You can't judge a book just by its cover. I'm not a real complicated man; I'm just your average joe, I've heard some many people say that to me.

If I had a penny for every time that I've heard that, I would be a millionaire if not a billionaire. All kidding aside, this garage door is jammed and won't open. How about you come in my house and go into the garage that way, that sounds like a good idea to me. I tell you what you go through my garage and get all your pictures and I will go check on Chris. You take care of Chris like he's your own kid, I don't want him to get any sicker then what he is. He's dead and his body is already beginning to decompose.

> "How much worse could he get?"

> "You got a point there, you don't need to check on him every hour."

He's always going to be in that cage and will always look the same, he stinks worse than a dead cow that's been rotting away for years. You should put an air freshener in your bedroom, and a fan. But he doesn't like it when the fan blows on him.

> "How do you know that?"

> "Because I have tried that and I stopped it because he did not like it."

> "He tried to hide his face when I turned the fan on."

> "Does the fan have a low and high switch?"

No, it's just a one speed cheap fan that I got from some store a year ago. I'm going to check on him anyway, suit yourself I will be taking pictures of the inside of the garage.

"If there's something in my way, would you mind if I moved it?"

"No"

Grayson walked into the middle of the garage, there was junk piled up to his shoulders. There were several card board boxes and there were old blankets that were wet and had mold growing all over them, it was a real shame. He let out a sneeze and went on taking pictures of the garage.

He quickly snapped two pictures of the left side and right sides of the garage. The walls of the garage were once white and we're now a dirty grayish color. He went to step over a box and just about tripped over a stuffed animal. It was a stuffed gorilla that remind him of a child hood character.

He looked in one of the boxes off to the left side of the garage and saw that there was a game controller that must have belonged to a game station. He saw that there was an towel lying on top of a box off to the right hand side of the garage.

There were several stink bugs all over the towel, there were a few holes in the towel. The stink bugs were crawling along and one of them was making a buzzing sound.

"How's Chris doing?"

"He's being grumpy again."

If you were a zombie you wouldn't be very happy either. I don't understand why don't you just kill Chris and bury him, that's what you should do.

"Are you crazy?"

"No"

I don't have a gun to shoot him with, and I could never kill him. Then he will keep on suffering just so you can be entertained by him. You have to be fair to him too. You need to think about what you are going to do with him.

"So did you take all of your pictures?"

"Yes," I did

I almost fell over some of the boxes, you're a hoarder and that's not a good thing. You need to get this garage and your house fixed up. This garage stinks like a garbage can.

You have boxes stacked up to the ceiling, and that's not how you put everything in order. You're a pack rat and need to make a complete turnaround or think about perminately closing this garage. I'll think about making changes to my garage.

"Does Chris have a leather collar around his neck?"

"No," and I would never put a collar around his ugly neck.

You should see if he will play fetch, like a dog. No he's not a dog, and I will treat him like I have been. His clothes are so ugly looking, and he's almost naked.

I hope that you're going to clean up the blood on the carpet in your bedroom, It looks like someone was murdered in your bedroom. This garage is so hot and stinky, all I can smell is the strong smell of cat pee and the smell of dead rotting stink bugs.

What else does it smell like, now don't talk smart to me, it also smells like mold. Your kids shouldn't be living in a mold infested house. They could get a respiratory infection and get complications from it.

"Don't you care about their health at all?"

"Yes"

I do care and never say that to me again.

"Is that understood?"

"Yes," it is.

I'm struggling through life and raising 2 kids isn't easy, you should try raising 2 kids when you have the time. I don't have much time to do what I have to do anyway.

"Do you live on your own?"

"No," I live with my father, who loves me very much.

At least you can live with your father, I don't have either parent anymore. They have passed away from cancer, a tear began to run down her cheek, and my mother was a real fighter but the cancer beat her on every twist and turn. My dad was the same way, I don't know how much more I can say about my parents, I'm crying and I don't like to cry in front of strangers.

"Would you like a hug?"

"No," thank you

I should be okay I just can't talk about my parents anymore today or I will cry again, now all my makeup is running down the both sides of my face.

"Do you need help wiping off the makeup?"

"No," I don't need any help.

"I will just use my hands to get the makeup off."

I feel like I've been at your house all, no you just have been here for little over 2 hours.

"How do you know that?"

"I timed you."

"How many pictures have you taken of my house?"

"I don't know, Probably 10 or 15."

"Did you take a picture of my flooded basement?"

"Yes," I did and I had to take the picture for my job."

You seem like you're so into your job, that you don't take much time for yourself. That's a true statement and I don't get out to meet new people that often. My dad always tells me that I work too much and don't get out enough. He's right, why don't you listen to him?

I'm so happy with my job, but if you get sick from working too much, then you can't work. I keep myself in good shape and I eat good. You need to rest to have a good next day. I sleep fine every night and if I had a zombie sleeping next to me like you do I would have night mares to the day I die.

You said that before, I know but that's how I feel about it. Consider yourself lucky that you don't have to sleep next to him. I'm lucky and you are the one who put Chris in your bedroom, so stop complaining.

You can put Chris in any other room in the house, you should put him in basement after you get the water out of it.

"Do you think he would be happier down in the basement?"

"I don't know"

"You're going to have to figure that out."

"What are you starring at?"

"I'm staring at the back of the garage door"

"What do you see?"

I'm looking at the world map on the back of the door and thinking about what my dad is doing.

"What's your dad doing?"

"I don't know I can't read his mind, he's probably in another town hall meeting."

"How often is he in a town hall meeting?"

"He goes once every week."

That's not very often, he must have an easy job. No, it's far from easy, trust me you wouldn't like his job not in the least bit. I've spent far too much time here, I want to get going. Before you go I want you to look at my bathroom sink.

"Why what's the matter with it?"

"It's all clogged up and I cannot get it unclogged."

I was wondering if you know anything about fixing a sink. I don't know everything about sinks, I'll look at it. Now be careful when walking down the hallway.

"What's Chris doing?"

"He's just being a typical zombie."

"How comes there are scratches all over your bedroom door?"

"Those scratches were from my cat"

I had closed the bedroom door and forget about him and we'll he decided to scratch the door until I let him out. I don't think the scratches in the door are that bad, yes they are, there are several deep scratches in the center of the door. I think that you should take this door down and get it replaced. This door looks terrible and the paint is beginning to peel off of it.

"How comes you have no door on the room next to your main bedroom?"

“I just haven't gotten around to it.”

Another excuse I should have known, you have an excuse for everything Kathleen. I know, I asked you to look closer at my sink not my bedroom door. Come in my bathroom and look in the sink.

“Is something going to jump up out of the sink at me?”

“No,” there's nothing hiding in my sink.

I heard that one before, there aren't just spiders and stink bugs hiding in your attic, there's a bat. I don't like bats, but the attic is so hot that If the bat doesn't find a way out he's not going to survive.

Chapter 8: Taking Things as they Come

I don't feel bad about the bat, I don't care about the bat or my attic. Alright your sink is dirty and I want you to wipe it down with a cloth before I even touch the drain or the sink.

“Why are you being such a neat freak?”

“I'm not”

I don't know what's in the sink, I just don't want to take a risk touching something that's contaminated. Next you're going to want me to get you a mask and bio hazard suit. Just stop right there, I'm not asking you to do much by wiping down the sink.

"Do you comb your hair, while standing in front of the sink?"

"Yes"

I look into the mirror every morning and run the comb through my hair. The problem is a lot of your hair has fell down into the drain and that could be the main reason why.

"Are you sure about that?"

"Yes"

It's just common sense, take a minute and think about it and you will realize that I'm right. I don't want to argue about why your sink is getting clogged. I suggest that you comb your hair away from the sink, But then I can't look into the mirror.

"Why do you have to make everything so complicated?"

"I don't know it's just part of my personality"

"Very funny, my head is beginning to hurt."

"What's wrong?"

"I'm getting a bad headache."

I'm getting frustrated and want to go home, don't be that way I didn't mean for my house to be in such bad shape. If I would of knew how bad of shape this house was I would of never appraised it and would have asked for demolition of this rat hole.

What this house isn't a rat hole, that's how you feel about it. Another thing I'm noticing is that the sink head has a slight leak to it, that means that the gaskets are wearing out in the sink fixture.

"How much would that cost?"

"I honestly cannot answer that question."

You may need to get the whole sink replaced. Alright so give me an average cost of a sink, it would cost upwards of $500 dollars. What! That's too much, forget about it. All I can hear is that rap music, please turn it down, and tell Chris that he has a bad taste of music.

"Why don't you play country music to him?"

"No," he only likes rap.

"Have you played country music for him before?"

No," and I don't like country music either, you're a tough customer.

Rap music is so violent, maybe Chris will calm down If you play classical music to him. I will try to play classical music to him and see what he does.

"When are you going to do that?"

"I'm going to do that after you leave."

Please don't bring up dating again and go out on a date.

"Do I look like I'm interested in dating you?"

"No," so don't bring it up again.

I about had it and just want to go, you can go at any time. I'm not holding you back, the toilet hasn't been flushing correctly, and seems like it's going to have a serious problem real soon. That's the last thing that I'm going to take a look at, I'm not a plumber but I will do what I can.

"How comes you are staying back away from the toilet so far."

"Do you know something that I don't?"

"Is something going to fly up out of the toilet bowl and hit me?"

"No," probably just some city water

The city water really stinks, and smells like they dumped too much chlorine into the city water.

"What's chlorine?"

"I don't know much about chlorine I'm sorry."

It's okay, and my white shower curtain is beginning to turn yellow.

"What could I spray on it to get it good and clean?"

"I would say just take some bleach and scrub it good with a rag."

I can't stand the smell of bleach, so please don't bring out the bleach while I'm in here or I will throw up.

"Are you going to be able to get the hair out of drain?"

"No," I cannot get it all out just some.

The rest you're going to have to get out by yourself, ghee thanks Grayson looked behind him and saw that Chris was sitting down gritting his teeth. All of his teeth were all yellow or had fallen out already.

There was blood running out the left side corner of his mouth, and he had a puzzled look on his. What's your problem? Stop looking at me you dumb zombie.

I don't have time to fix this house you dumb zombie, now look the other way. Chris didn't listen and began to growl and moan. I can't stand it when you growl you silly zombie. I think now I'm ready to go.

"Is there anything else in this lousy house you want me to look at?"

"Yes," there's one more thing I want you to look at.

"Where is it?"

"It's this light fixture in my kitchen, I will look at it."

"What seems to be the problem with it?"

"It lights up by then turns off, and flickers a lot."

That just means that you have to get the bulb replaced. Suddenly Chris stood up and began to shake the cage and had an angry look on his face and he growled louder than he had in a while. I think something's wrong with him, he won't calm down, I don't understand what happened to him.

"What should I do to make him calm down?"

"Give him the teddy bear that is sitting on the chair beside his cage."

I didn't know that zombies liked to cuddle with a teddy bear. He does, I never thought that zombies cuddle with things. See that you're learning more about zombies, I don't know if that's a good or bad thing.

"How many teddy bears has he ripped up?"

"He's ripped up 2, before and this is the last one that I will ever buy him."

He just put the small brown teddy bear under his chin and is now acting like he's going to fall asleep. Don't look at him while he's sleeping or he'll wake up in a rage and scary you.

"Is he grumpy all of the time or just when I'm around?"

"He doesn't know you too well that's why he keeps acting out."

"How's he supposed to get to know me?"

"Just remain in the room for a few more minutes."

"Do you want me here all day long?"

"No"

I get lonely and have been looking for a good loving man to stay with me and Chris.

"Who was the man that you had your kids with?"

"I'm trying to forget about him"

His name was Oscar and he was Mexican and Native American, and had some Irish in him. He treated me good for many years but I found out that he was cheating on me with the women at the local grocery store.

"How do you know that?"

"One day I followed him into the grocery store without him, knowing."

I hid behind the isles as I walked along watching him, it turns out that he was having a secret relationship with one of the cashiers.

"Do you remember what the women's name was?"

"No," I don't and I don't care what her name is anymore.

"How long was he with her for?"

"I have no idea."

Be good and stop trying to rip the head off of the teddy bear, you will not get another teddy bear if you don't behave yourself. Don't give me that stupid look, you're no dumb zombie. Stop trying to rip the Bears legs off.

Don't you dare start eating the bear, suddenly he picked up the bear and tried to shove the whole thing in his mouth. Stop it Chris, don't eat the teddy bear. Would you please try to help me make him to stop eating the bear. Here throw this pillow at the cage.

"Why would I do that?"

"Maybe it would make him stop eating the teddy bear."

I'm getting tired of watching this zombie. Here take the pillow back, and you throw the pillow at your zombie. I won't and if I had a gun with me I would shoot that zombie and take him out of his misery.

"Do you have a gun?"

"No."

I don't want anyone to shoot my zombie. He's mine all mine and if I want him to suffer then he will suffer, you're showing me how self-centered you really are.

"How can you stand it in here?"

"I don't know I have a small window air conditioner that runs all day."

"Why don't you just get central air put in?"

"I haven't thought about that but I will look into after today."

Alright, I have just decided that I want to stay here for as long as it will take you to tell me the story about Chris. Now please start telling about him.

One day a friend of mine gave me a call and told me that one of the people that he worked with had died in a chemical accident. His name was Chris, now my friend was very upset that his coworker had died from his injures. My friend said that there was a pond nearby that was full of chemicals and biohazard waste.

Chris had to walk across a bride that crossed over the pond and the bridge was slippery and this caused him to lose his balance and well he fell into the contaminated pond.

He said that Chris was flopping around in the water like a fish, and he kept asking for help and he didn't know how to swim. So why didn't your friend help him, because he wasn't going to jump into the pond.

After a short Chris was floating on the surface of the water head down in the water. He had passed away and my friend said that he must have cried for ten minutes.

An hour passed and he called the local Fire Company, and they used their ladder truck and were able to get him out of the pond. His body was all stiff and some of his flesh was coming off of his face and hands.

"How come the coroner hasn't come?"

"He did but my friend said that he wanted the body because he was an organ donor and that he would bring the body back to the morgue and the guy was okay with it."

"What did your friend do next?"

"He found a large cage and was able to get his body into it."

"He locked it up and waited there for an hour"

"How did he know that he was going to wake up and live as a zombie?"

"He didn't know"

He put his body in the cage so that no animals would start feeding on his dead body. 2 hours went by and Chris woke up and he said that he tried to talk to him but he just kept on moaning and groaning.

My friend called me and asked me about if I thought from what he was telling me about Chris if he was a zombie or not. I told him that he was a zombie then he asked me if I wanted a zombie as a pet and I said yes. The next day, he came over with Chris and we decided to place him in my bedroom. You should have put him in the basement, and been done with it. I agree with that but he's staying in my room.

I'm going to leave now, good luck with that zombie named Chris.

Grayson quickly walked down the hall way and out of the house through the front door. Kathleen followed him out and said bye.

Grayson quickly got in his car and wasted no time getting out of there. He was driving a bit over the speed limit but it didn't bother him at all. He thought to himself that house was absolutely just terrible. He checked his cell phone and there was a message on it.

It was his dad and he said that he was going to have to spend an extra hour at work and that he would be home when he could. Grayson thought to himself my dad's always so busy.

He decided to turn onto a back street that went past the woods, all of a sudden a young turkey came walking along onto the street and Grayson had to slam on his brakes to avoid running over the turkey.

He waited a moment and the turkey crossed the road and was now on the other side. Grayson let out a sigh and continued on. He looked at the clock on the dash and it showed that it was 2:45. After 20 minutes he got to his office and he could see that his boss was standing out in the parking lot.

He carefully pulled into a parking space that was near where his boss was standing. He looked over at his boss and noticed that was holding his cell phone up to his ear and he was talking very loudly. Grayson opened the driver's side door and stood up and turned to face his boss. His boss didn't even notice him until he was right in front him.

"How are you doing?"

"I'm doing good"

"What took you so long to get back to the office from the job."

"How about you come in my office Mr. Lloyd and I'll tell you about it?"

"That sounds good to me, just let me get off of the phone and I will join you."

20 minutes later Mr. Lloyd came into his office and carefully sat down. Grayson took his time and began to tell him the story and the secretary came into the room and said excuse me but we need to talk, alright I'll be back in a few minutes. Grayson put his head down on his desk and fell asleep.

Mr. Lloyd came into the room, and the secretary wasn't with him this time. He couldn't believe that Grayson had fallen asleep so quickly, he patted him on the shoulder to see if that would wake him up.

When he woke up he saw that Mr. Lloyd was looking at him with a disgusted look on his face. You fall asleep quicker than anyone I know, you shouldn't be sleeping so much.

"What happened to the secretary?"

"She quit."

I'm not happy about what happened, it was a bad argument. A man with blood all over his body came over to the window, they both looked at each other and screamed zombie. That looks like the zombie that the woman had the bedroom, maybe he just escaped.

"Do you think I should shoot him?"

"No."

Mr. Lloyd pulled out his gun and shot the man, and the bullet shattered the window. You didn't shoot him in the head, so chances are he'll be getting up again.

I hope that you're wrong, the zombie slowly got back up and slowly lumbered over to them. He looked at the both of them, I can't believe that he's looking at us. The zombie kept his eyes on Mr. Lloyd, he's looking at you instead of me.

"Which one of you shot me asked the zombie?"

"Mr. Lloyd replied I did."

You fellas won't have to worry about me I'm a good zombie.

"What's your name zombie?"

"Chris."

When I got out of the cage, it scared the person who was taking care of me and they ran away. It took me a while to figure out how to get out of the house.

I broke down the front door, and escaped out to the street. As I was walking down the street, a man saw me and ran away. I didn't mean to scare the man, I guess my bad looks scare people. You really need to wipe your eyes, there's blood dripping down from them.

Grayson took out a Kleenex from his pocket and handed it to Chris. He wiped his eyes and mouth, then threw it on the floor. You don't have good manners, you don't just throw things on the floor.

Grayson happened to look over at Mr. Lloyd, and noticed that he was lying flat on the floor. He quickly went over to him, and saw that he was still breathing. His eyes were closed, but one of his hands were twitching.

He thought to himself oh great just what we need another zombie. Chris was staring at him, if you're just going to sit there and not help me then get out of here.

"Did you hear what I said?"

"Yes."

If I call an ambulance, you better get out of here before they get here.

"Why?"

"Because you'll scare them."

Stop trying to eat my shoe, and think. A man with an assault rifle came walking down the street, and he spotted Chris. The man yelled out get out of there, I'm going to shoot that zombie for you.

I'm not going to ask you again, Grayson came out of the building. Come closer to me, so I can pat you down. There's nothing on me that could be a danger to you, I'm just making sure.

Look the zombie is trying to eat that man on the ground, stop trying to hold me up. If I don't shoot that zombie now he'll eat that man, it's not what you think. The zombie is friendly, he doesn't look very friendly to me.

If you go over there he'll talk to you, I've never heard of a zombie talking before. The man ignored what Grayson said, and started shooting Chris. If you try to take my gun from me I'll shoot you as well.

Grayson could hear police sirens and took off through the parking lot until he reached his car, he quickly got in it and started it up. He drove out of the parking lot, and onto the road. As he was driving along, someone walked out of the woods and onto the road.

He quickly slammed on the brakes, and came to a complete stop. A woman with blood coming out of her ears and mouth came over to him.

You realize that I could have hit you, and you shouldn't be in the woods. I know that you don't care if you get run over because you're a zombie but I care.

"Where are you headed?"

"To the grocery store."

You won't be finding a grocery store in the woods, it's the only place where I feel safe. Everyone in the town sees me and runs away, and the police shoot at me. A while ago a rabid fox took a bite out of me, and ran off. Us zombies have no rights, and were constantly being attacked.

We should at least have rights, then you should go to the Supreme Court. There's no way that I'm going to go there, the guards would shoot me down. Then you should wear a mask, and clean the blood off of your body.

I tried to do that last week, and it didn't go so well for me. My skin came off, and it made me sick. You're a zombie those things shouldn't bother you, I know a joke if you'd like to hear it, go ahead.

"What do they call a wondering zombie?"

"A walker."

That question was too easy, you'll have to ask more difficult questions next time. I was trying to find a movie the other night, and kept coming across action movies with zombies being killed in them. I was horrified by what I was seeing, I had to close my eyes for some of the scenes. Millions of zombies must have died in those movies, I'm not so sure about that.

These days they have computer animation that creates fictional characters in movies. When I was alive, I was working as a model. I was so beautiful back then, now my body is ugly and it's wasting away. I heard on the news, that tomorrow is voting day.

I'm not going to go vote, because I'd scared everyone away. You won't if you cover yourself up, rap a scarf around your neck. Put on gloves, and spray plenty of perfume all over your body. I must have lost almost all my hair, and it's not growing back. I used to play with my hair, and I enjoyed braiding it.

> "Can you still drive?"

> "No," I've forgotten how to do it.

> "Have you ever saw a zombie drive?"

> "No."

2 weeks ago I tried to buy a lottery ticket at the gas station, and the guy behind the counter ran away and so did the other people that were there. The man called the Police, and before they got there I walked off. People act like I'm going to eat them or something, and I even told them

that I was a good zombie. The other day I was very hungry for some ice cream, so I went over to the ice cream shop.

The minute I walked in the place, everyone screamed it's a zombie. That wasn't very nice of them to say to me, then when I went to order my ice cream they threw ice cream at me.

I was covered in ice cream, and they were laughing at me. I figured that I'd scare them and growled at them, they immediately got down behind the counter. They stopped laughing, and had serious looks on their faces. In the end I lucked out, because I got free ice cream.

"Did they call the Police on you?"

"No."

The minute that I walked out of the door, the people came out from behind the counter. I tried to get on a bus, but the driver wouldn't open the doors to let me get in.

When I went to the bank and tried to withdraw money from my account, someone came out from behind the counter and pepper sprayed me. The person yelled at me get out of here zombie, and gave me a swift kick as I was walking out.

After all of this happened to me, I made my own protesting sign. I stood outside the Governor's mansion and held up my sign, until the guards came out and shot me full of holes. Then I quickly ran off, and hid in an abandoned building.

"Did the guards come looking for you there?"

"No."

I'm really hungry for some nachos and cheese right now, I can't help you with that. It's been nice talking with you, and he speed off. An hour later he got home, and laid down in his bed and soon after fell asleep.